make your own magic

the ST⊙RYTELLERS RULE

by Christy Mandin

HARPER
An Imprint of HarperCollinsPublishers

One morning, the Storytellers assembled.

All right, gather 'round. I've called this emergency meeting because we have a crisis of imagination on our hands.

amazing ideas jar

As you know, it was a big year.
A new school.
A new and very loud baby brother.
Homework.

MAY
S M T W TH F S

CREATIVE WRIT
PROJECT

Create your ow
using your

BONUS: Add ill

DUE ... Y 26th

BLUE'S
old-fashioned
Jumping beans

The closer we get to the end of the school year, the more Birdie is struggling to be creative.

She used to love writing and making up fun characters, but she can't seem to get past the blank page anymore.

And we have the big end-of-year writing assignment to worry about.

I don't think I can take much more sharpening and nervous chewing. Homework is wrecking me. I'll completely disappear if we don't do something!

Pip was right. They had to do something.

Ahem. I know this is an emergency and we are pressed for time, but can we please abide by the rules and recite the guidelines of the Storytellers, as is tradition?

How about when she found the perfect rock in the park?!

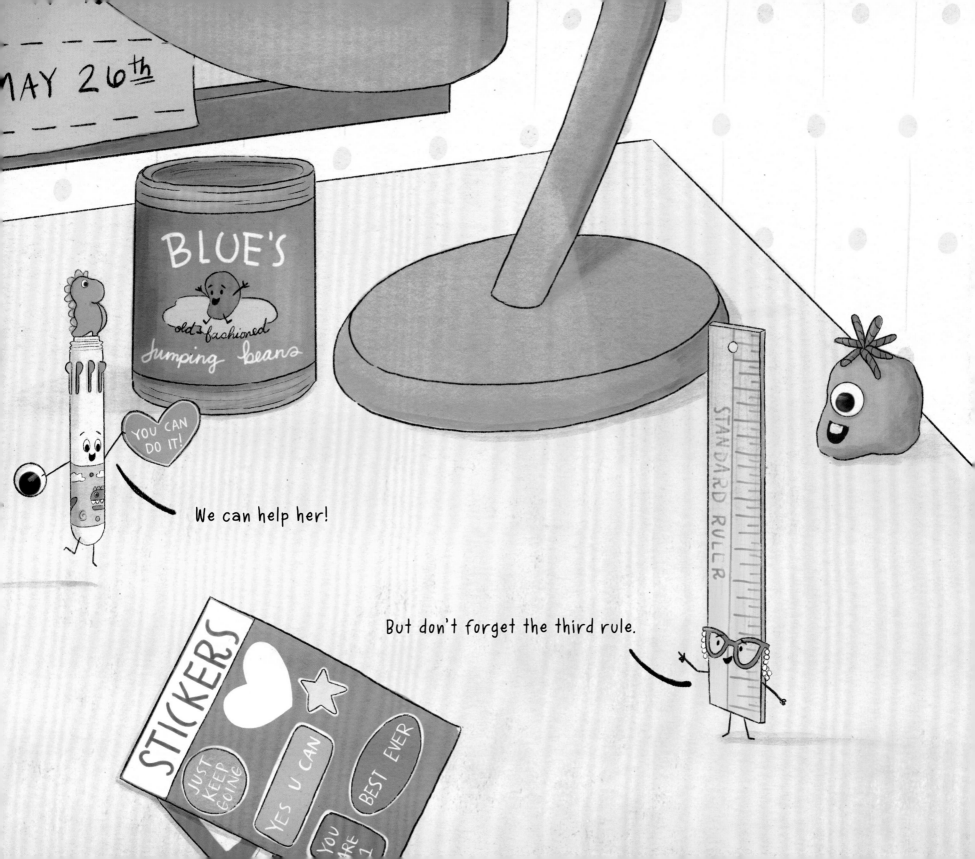

They talked some more
and came up with a plan.

That night, after Birdie fell asleep, the Storytellers got to work.

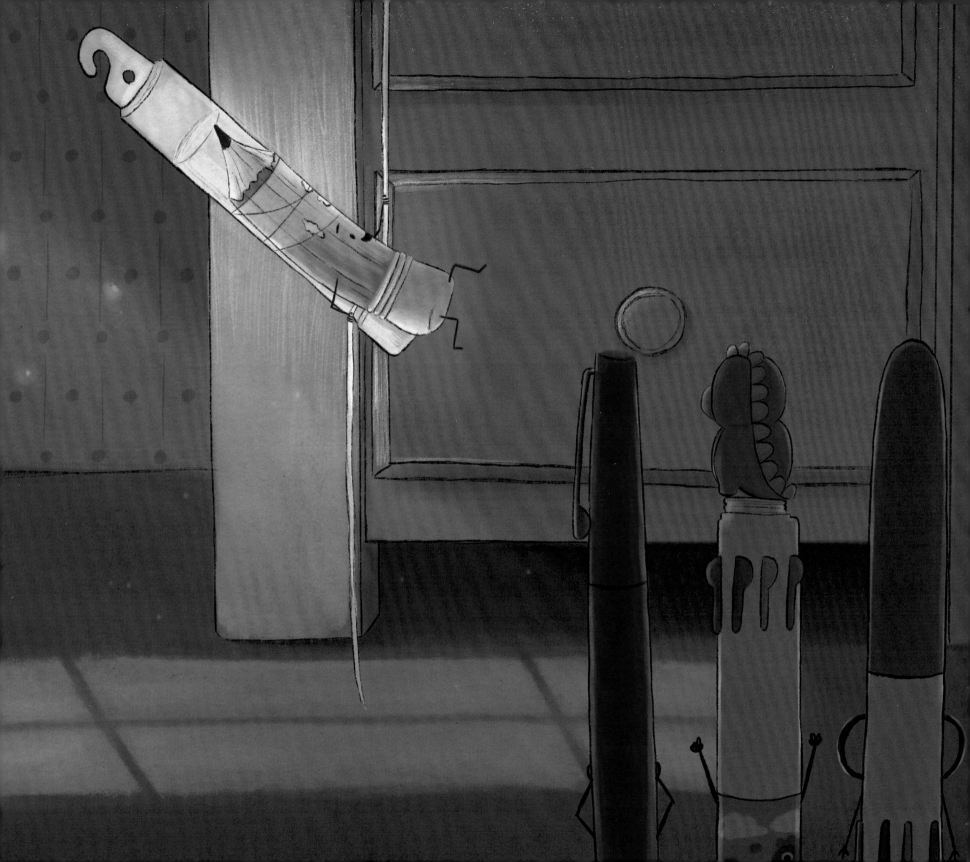

They cleverly arranged this . . .

. . . and that.

And hopped back in their cups before the sun came up.

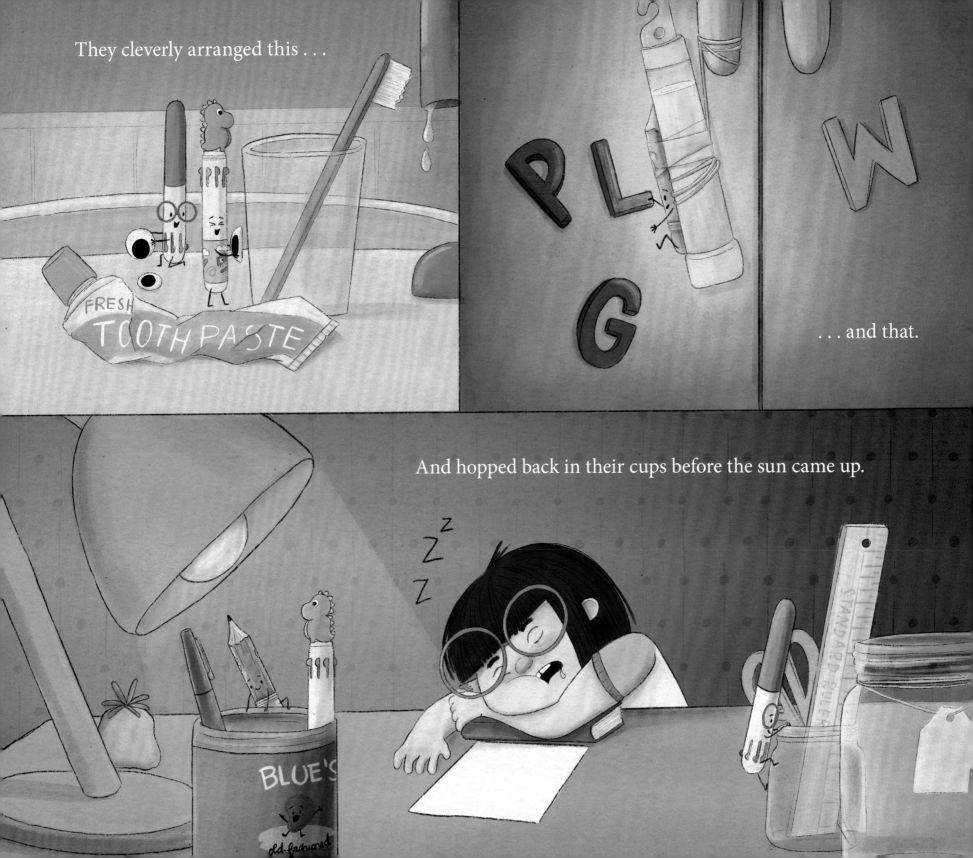

Birdie woke with a jolt.

She'd fallen asleep at her desk
without writing a thing . . . again.

At first they weren't sure if Birdie would even notice their clues.

But then, a spark.

A light bulb.

The next thing they knew, the Storytellers were on a walk, making lists, feverishly jotting things down.

One idea led to another, and suddenly the world all around came to life in a fresh way.

Birdie had an idea jar full of ideas, a notebook full of lists,

a tin full of words, and a head full of characters.

But no stories. Despite all her heart maps and quick writes and sketching, Birdie had only ended up with bits and pieces of stories.

She started to feel defeated yet again by her nemesis, the blank page.

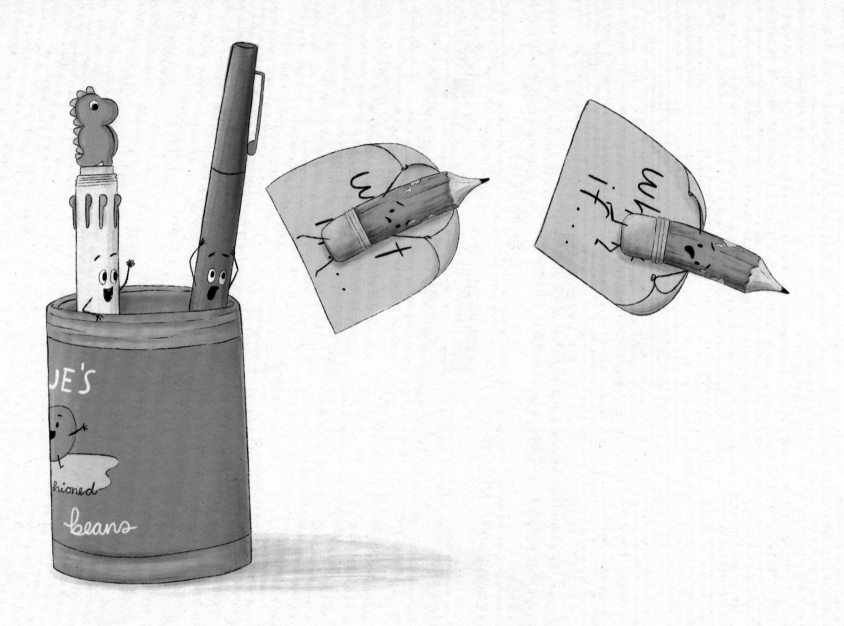

Desperate, Pip broke the Storytellers' oath
and leaped from her cup onto the desk.

The pencil caught Birdie's eye, and she wondered.

The more she wondered, the more her imagination grew.

She started to connect the dots of things she liked.

As Birdie held tight to her inner voice,
the words flowed out from her mind,
through her hand, and onto the paper.

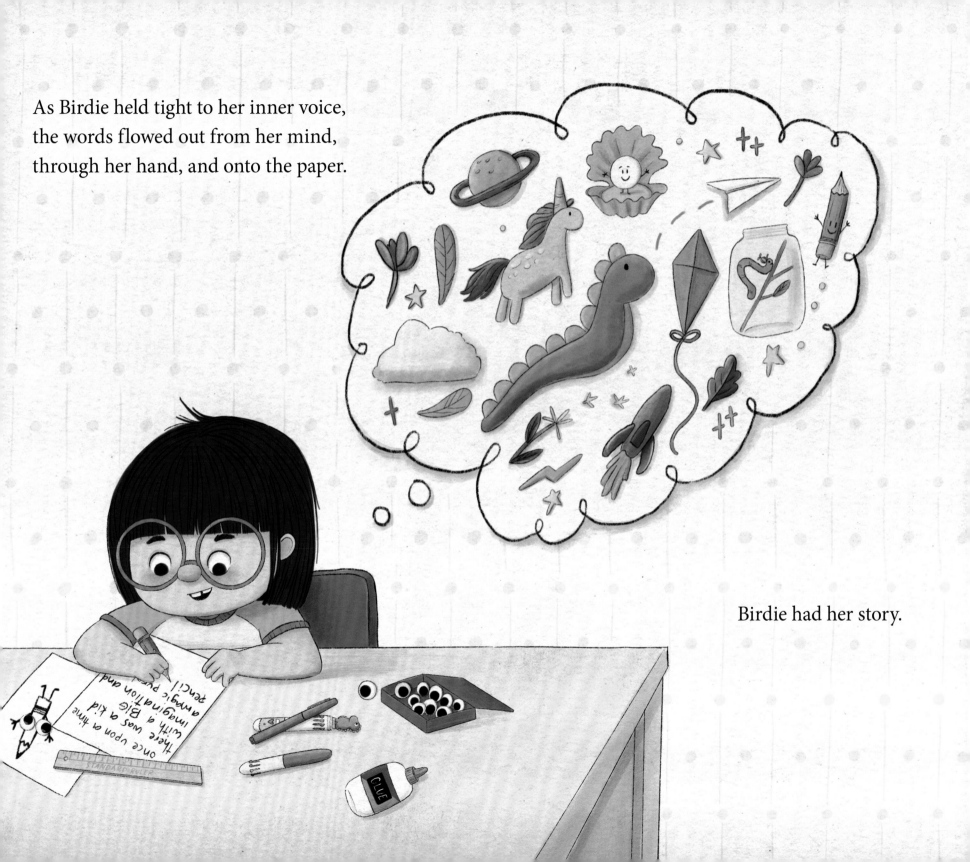

Birdie had her story.

And now, anytime Birdie has trouble with a blank page,

she keeps a note to remember the most important rule of storytelling:

always begin with wonder

ABOUT THIS BOOK

Library on Congress Control Number: 2022931784
ISBN 978-0-06-304735-8

The artist used Procreate to create the digital illustrations for this book.
Typography by Christy Mandin and Chelsea C. Donaldson
22 23 24 25 26 RTLO 10 9 8 7 6 5 4 3 2 1
❖
First Edition

FOR LUANA, ADRIA,
AND CHELSEA.

THANK YOU FOR GUIDING
ME AND HELPING ME
MAKE MAGIC.